Rungle
IN THE
Jungle

By Robert Logan Rogers
Illustrated by Rachel McCoy

I want to dedicate this book to my illustrator Rachel who created, out of the soul of my story, characters with color and life! Also to my three children, Jessica, Joshua, and Timothy.

— Robert Logan Rogers

RUNGLE
IN THE
JUNGLE

By Robert Logan Rogers

Illustrated by Rachel McCoy

Timmy was a fearless tiger
He loved to drink his apple cider
Dreaming he would be a fighter
Sparring with his friend the spider

Joshua was a jumping jaguar
Who played a game of tug-o-war
For him to pull was not a chore
As he wrestled with a boar

Jessica was a tall giraffe
Who loved to take a bubble bath
Her legs were like a shepherd's staff
She loved to giggle, then loved to laugh

One day while playing in the jungle
They began to toss and tumble
As the grass began to crumble
Josh declared without a mumble

Today I declare
He said with a smile
Let's have a race
And run for a mile

Let's call the tall
And some who are small
Some who will crawl
And some who play ball

The big and the fast
Will make up the cast
Let's call a bird
To send out the word

We will make it a day
So what do you say
All are invited
So let's get excited

A perch for a search
On Jessica's neck
Like a mast from a ship
They reached from her deck

Because she was
As tall as the trees
She would help find
The strongest of knees

An elephant was found
Enjoying the sun
They asked would he come
To join in this run

He said with a smile
All over his face
I'll find even more
To come to this race

They happened upon
A big lion napping
Who'd just finished singing
A song he was rapping

Would the king of the beasts
Like to come to this race
Singing his tune
And setting the pace

Indeed I would
I'd hardly be trying
No one can beat me
For I am the lion

The race will begin
As we gather together
I will roar to the wind
And pray for good weather

Excited they parted
Bumping into a rhino
Who said with a smile
Just where do I sign—o

It seemed they had gathered
Enough to begin
When out popped an ape
Declaring his win

A gorilla I am
Weighing more than a ton
I'll lose me some weight
Before starting this run

Now everyone thought
That they would prevent
The others from winning
This momentous event

But no one had thought
That across from the lake
Crawling and sneering
Would enter the snake

Appearing before them
He started to boast
This is no race
For me it's a coast

As long as I am
From beginning to end
I will beat one and all
Before reaching the bend

He caused such a stir
For those who were entered
That fear was now focused
As fear would be centered

This slithery crook
With all of his slime
Used fear as his hook
To pull off his crime

The picture he painted
Would help to defeat
The image they had
Of moving their feet

This master's illusion
Had all of them worried
He played with their minds
And he never was hurried

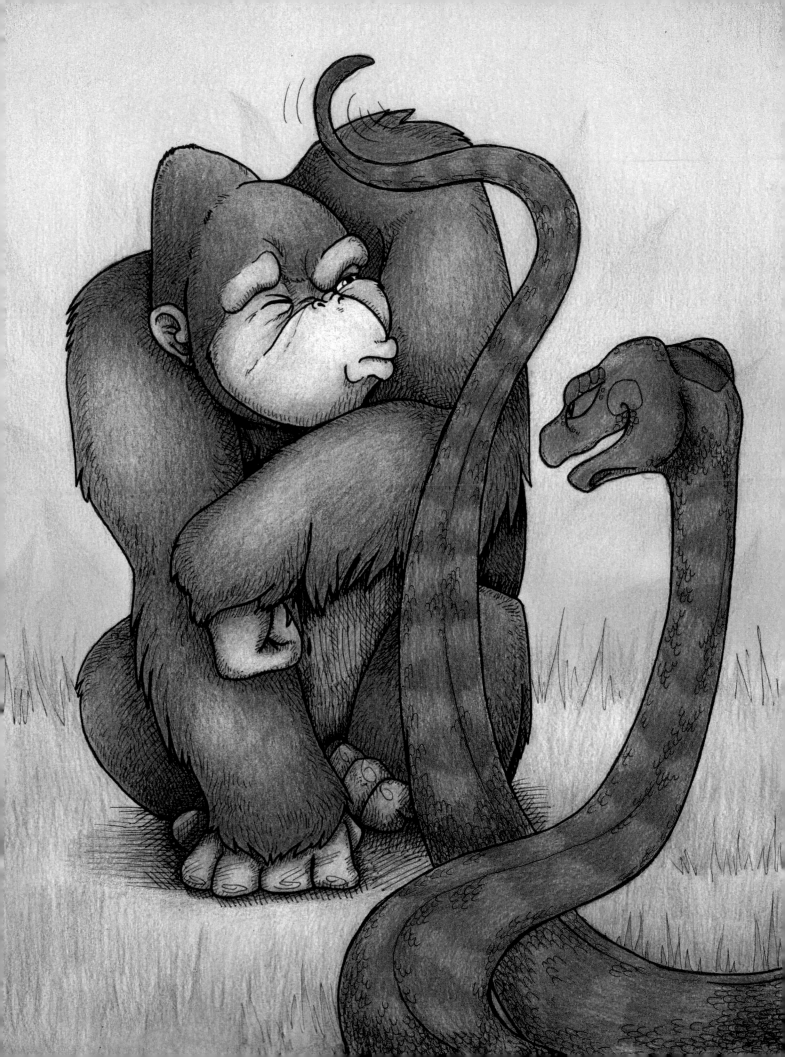

But then there was Josh
With his buddy Tim
They just finished having
A mid—morning swim

With hardly a care
They paid no attention
To this cunning deception
With no good intention

Unlike the others
Who started to listen
To all of this chatter
The snake was a—hissin'

The boys were just smarter
As they took out a plug
To cover their ears
From hearing this thug

For inside their heads
The noise was now covered
While positive thoughts
Would soon be discovered

As the day of the race
Finally was here
Zebras and monkeys
Began to appear

All of the animals
Formed a parade
Turtles were selling
Cold lemonade

All of the magic
Was there for the gang
It soon would begin
With the sound of a bang

As they got ready
And lined up to start
Each of them knew
They all played a part

The boys were excited
As they entered the race
Leading the pack
And setting the pace

While the runners got ready
In the air all could tell
They all were unsteady
As the snake cast his spell

Boasting again
He repeated his claim
No one can beat me
You can 't win this game

Your mark get set
And ready to go
A blast for this cast
Had started the show

Then suddenly the snake
While grabbing his tail
Soon formed a wheel
And started to sail

Leaving behind
All the animals running
Picking up speed
His move was so cunning

Without any thought
For what looked so slick
The boys were just humored
By this little trick

Rolling like thunder
The snake gained his speed
Rounding each corner
He started to lead

Then all of a sudden
Singing loop—tee—loop
The boys used the snake
For their traveling hoop

He opened his mouth
And started to hiss
He flattened right out
As they blew him a kiss

Like a tire that's flat
On the side of the road
This broken down snake
Was a traveling load

Coughing and spewing
The dust from his nose
He sort of resembled
A broken down hose

I'll get you he cried
As he started to squirm
Then a bird picked him up
Thinking he was a worm

Cheers were so loud
From the sound of the crowd
They all got a lift
From the boys' little gift

Their joy brought a smile
As they finished the mile
Laughing along
They all sang a song

Victory is sweet
While moving our feet
We all have a song
To right every wrong

So the boys won the race
With big smiles on their face
As they finished their lap
With a victory nap

So they started to snore
While dreaming once more
Of their run in the sun
Which had been so much fun

So champions can be
Big hearts of gold
Children with fears
Must always be told

That snakes are as crafty
As you let them be
If you look past your fear
You will always be free

The End

Acknowledgements

I want to thank some very special people who helped me and encouraged me during the process of writing and rewriting the verses to this story. First of all Norine my wife, who brought her unique laugh and animated reactions to the table, every time I read the story to a new group of friends or family. Her constant encouragement to pursue excellence made me move in deliberation and determination.

I also want to thank the young people in Corning, New York who, in 2012, insisted that I pick the manuscript up one more time and complete the project.

I also want to thank the many who prayed for its completion. Thanks Ginny, Peggy, and Stacey! You guys kept the snake in check!

Blessings to all of you,
Logan

For more Rungle in the Jungle goodies visit
rungleinthejunglethebook.com!

Comments? Questions? Contact
Logan Rogers at **rungleinthejungle@gmail.com**.

Made in the USA
San Bernardino, CA
02 March 2015